TEAM SUPERCREW presents

BENNY THE BRAVE IN

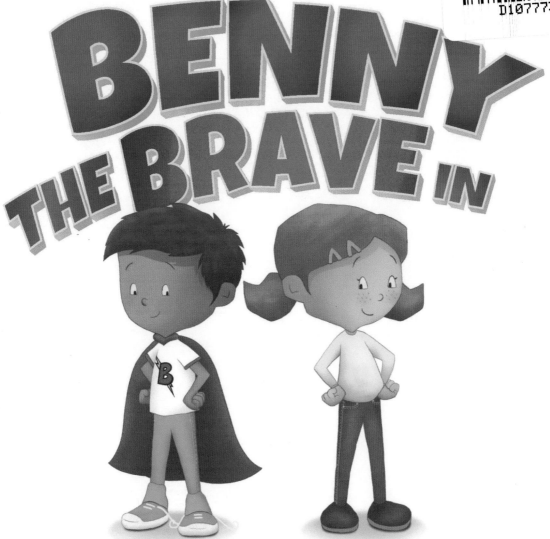

THE FIRST DAY JITTERS

By **Julie Anne Penn** and **Darren Penn** Illustrated by **Sergio De Giorgi**

For BB...our greatest teacher

\- J.P. and D.P.

For April, Emma, and Vivi—my superheroes

\- S.D.G

ISBN: 979-8-9854707-0-3

First edition, 2022

Cover Designer: Jess Lam
Editor: Lauren Kerstein

A special thanks to Jamie Schrager, Psy.D., Kristen Piering, Psy.D.,
Amanda Lupis, Kimberley Mauro, Ella, Jack, and Felix.

Team Supercrew Be Extraordinary is a trademark of Supercrew Incorporated.

www.teamsupercrew.com

WE'RE TEAM SUPERCREW! Superhero kids with awesome abilities: the power to be kind, the power to be brave, the power of grit, and the power to be calm. We help kids find their own powers when they need them most. Want to join us?

Benny the Brave   Keisha the Kind   Chloe the Calm   Gen the Grit

"I don't want to go to school today."

"It's my first day, Benny."

"The bus will be here in five minutes, Honey.
I'll meet you by the front door, lickety-split!"

"Oh, Benny. I wish you could come with me."

"I...am...scared."

"What's happening?"

"Whoa! Benny. What? How...? I must be dreaming."

"Hey, Sarah. Did you say you're scared?"

"You called me and I came! As a proud member of
Team Supercrew, I, Benny the Brave am here to help.
Why are you scared?"

my new school is so far away."

"I feel scared because...

2 + 3 = 5
4 − 2 = 2
6 − 5 = 1

my teacher will have gigantic teeth and a long, slimy tail."

my lunch will be squirmy and squishy and gross!"

"I feel scared because...

I am new and nobody will want to play with me."

"It's okay to feel scared.

But...what if..."

"You love adventures!"

"What if...

Mom packed your favorite cheese sandwich. And look, a chocolate-chip cookie. The big one!"

"What if...

"Yes! You are brave and you can do anything! As a brave friend of Team Supercrew, you now have the power inside of you whenever you need it."

"What if...

It's always been there."

WANT TO BUILD YOUR SUPERHERO SKILLS?

Next time you need a bravery boost, try these four simple steps:

1. Notice how you're feeling. Are you feeling scared? Worried? Nervous? Lonely? All of these feelings are okay, and lots of kids (and adults, too!) experience them all the time.

2. Share your thoughts and feelings with a trusted adult or friend.

3. Try to change your thoughts so they are more positive or hopeful. You might even think about a time you showed bravery before. Friends and adults can help you with this part.

4. Notice how you're feeling now. Did the feeling change?

Your thoughts create your feelings! You now have the power to think brave thoughts and show bravery whenever you need it, just like **Benny and Sarah!**

Want to make your own Brave Book? Scan the QR code for your free Brave Book template!

Printed in Great Britain
by Amazon